PATRICIA FORDE

To the Island

Illustrated by
NICOLA BERNARDELLI

Little Island

Galway 2020 Gaillimh   European Capital of Culture

Fia looked out over the bay, hoping to see the island.

Hy Brasil! That's what it was called, the mysterious island.
It sounded like an ancient spell or a prayer.

It only appeared
once every
seven years.

Fia longed
to go there.

That night, when the moon was high –
higher than the fishing boats,
higher than the church steeple –
she crept out of her warm bed
and went down to the quay.

The wind whistled through the streets as Fia made her way to the old stone arch.

The sea was calm.
The mountains crouched
like giants in the distance.

Mist swirled itself about Fia.

Come away!
it seemed to say.
Come away!

Fia felt the pull of magic in the air
and the pull of her own strong heart.
She put one foot on the water.

A silver moonbeam stretched
beneath her feet,
leading her out into the light.

She hopped from star to star
and then she stopped –
and there it was –

Hy Brasil!

Rising out of the waves,
graceful as a whisper.

Fia stepped onto the island,
where the air was thick with secrets.

Magical creatures strode about,
their coats glistening, voices echoing.

Fia stood in the shade of the dripping rock.
She washed her face in the heather water
and her skin was freckled with silver drops.

She rode on the back of a gilded butterfly
and felt his heartbeat next to hers.

Then out of the tower
came a host of boys and girls
Dancing! Twirling!
Swooping in and out.

A boy with eyes like summer puddles
took Fia's hand, and she danced too.

She danced and danced till her head spun
and her feet hardly touched the ground.

The dance took Fia to the bed of the sea, where messages lurked in bottles and old gold gleamed in pirates' chests.

She danced up to the
clear night sky where
wishes are pinned to stars,
and stardust tickled her nose
and painted her lips with silver.

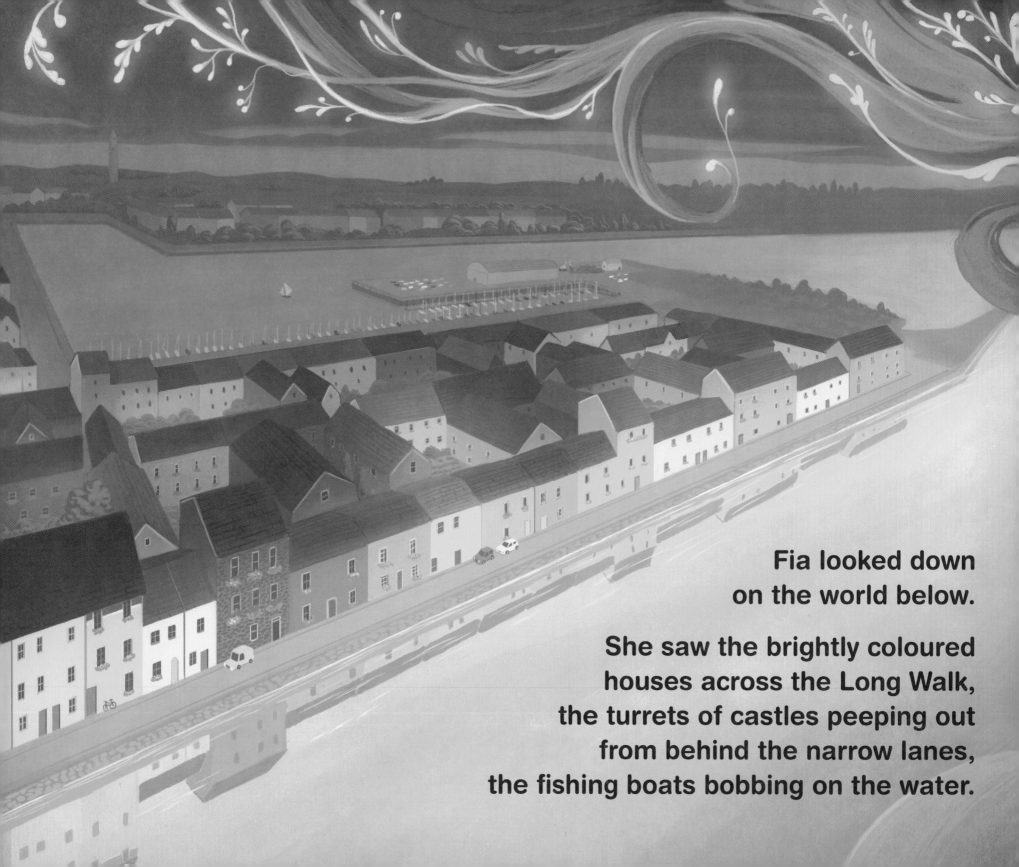

Fia looked down
on the world below.

She saw the brightly coloured
houses across the Long Walk,
the turrets of castles peeping out
from behind the narrow lanes,
the fishing boats bobbing on the water.

Over the moonbeam, through the stars,
Fia stepped till ghostly white swans peeped
through the mist and she felt the ground
once more beneath her feet.

Fia looked back one last time.

She saw Hy Brasil looming over the waves while the other islands and the distant hills looked on in wonder.

Then slowly,

oh so slowly,

Hy Brasil slipped

beneath the sea.

Fia turned and ran.

She ran through the twisting narrow streets, following the compass of her own small heart.

All the way home.

About Patricia Forde

Patricia Forde is from Galway, on the west coast of Ireland. Patricia has published several picture books in Irish and English, as well as three novels for children, published by Little Island Books. She has won two White Raven awards and has twice been shortlisted for the Children's Books Ireland Book of the Year. *Bumpfizzle the Best on Planet Earth* was the Dublin UNESCO Citywide Read 2019. *The Wordsmith* was published as *The List* in North America and is a Library Association of America Notable Book for Children. Patricia is married to Padraic and has two grown up children. She still lives in Galway, her favourite city in the world.

About Nicola Bernardelli

Nicola Bernardelli is an illustrator from Verona, Italy. He is a graduate of the Emile Cohl School of art in Lyon, France. He loves to depict nature, and the timeless human traits expressed in mythology and fairy tales.

About Little Island

Little Island Books publishes good books for young minds –
from toddlers all the way up to older teens. Based in Dublin,
Little Island was founded in 2010. We are a small, independent
press with a particular commitment to working with Irish authors
and illustrators, and we also publish some books in translation.
For more details about Little Island Books, please visit
www.littleisland.ie.

About This Book

To the Island is published by Little Island Books and was
commissioned by Galway 2020 European Capital of Culture.
In 2020, Galway in the West of Ireland (together with Rijeka in
Croatia) is the European Capital of Culture. This book forms part
of the Galway 2020 programme and celebrates Galway children's
author Patricia Forde's love of islands, real and imaginary. Italian
artist Nicola Bernardelli was selected as illustrator. Look out for
events connected with *To the Island* throughout the Galway 2020
programme and beyond – as well as a song called 'To the Island'
by Galway singer Anna Mullarkey, downloadable from
www.littleisland.ie!

Little Island

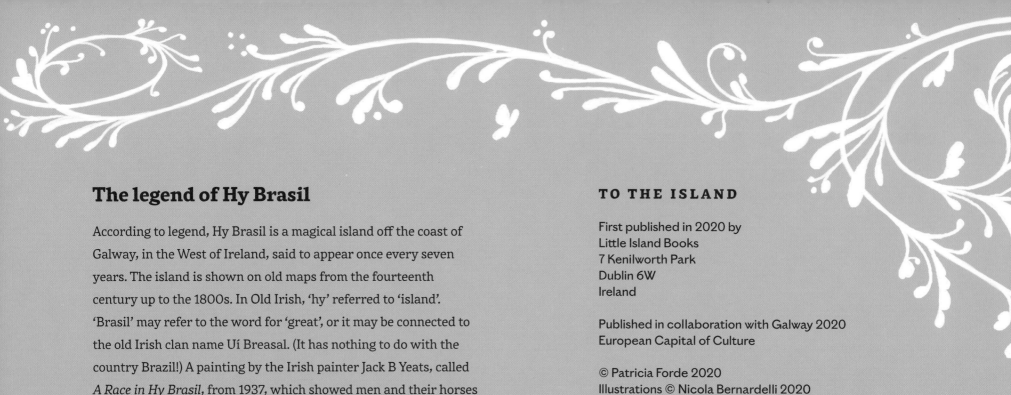

The legend of Hy Brasil

According to legend, Hy Brasil is a magical island off the coast of Galway, in the West of Ireland, said to appear once every seven years. The island is shown on old maps from the fourteenth century up to the 1800s. In Old Irish, 'hy' referred to 'island'. 'Brasil' may refer to the word for 'great', or it may be connected to the old Irish clan name Uí Breasal. (It has nothing to do with the country Brazil!) A painting by the Irish painter Jack B Yeats, called *A Race in Hy Brasil*, from 1937, which showed men and their horses getting ready for a race on the mythical island. In the nineteenth century, Irish poet Gerald Griffin wrote a poem about the island, which contained the lines:

On the ocean that hollows the rocks where ye dwell

A shadowy land has appeared, as they tell;

Men thought it a region of sunshine and rest,

And they called it Hy-Brasail, the isle of the blest;

From year unto year, on the ocean's blue rim,

The beautiful spectre showed lovely and dim;

The golden clouds curtained the deep where it lay,

And it looked like an Eden, away, far away!

TO THE ISLAND

First published in 2020 by
Little Island Books
7 Kenilworth Park
Dublin 6W
Ireland

Published in collaboration with Galway 2020
European Capital of Culture

ISBN: 978-1-912417-51-3

Designed by Niall McCormack
Art directed by Claire Brankin
Printed in Bosnia and Herzegovina by Imago

10 9 8 7 6 5 4 3 2 1